Happy Easter, Everyone!

A Lift-the-Flap Story

by Hopi Morton
illustrated by Robert Powers

Based on the TV series Little Bill® created by Bill Cosby as seen on Nick Jr.®

Simon Spotlight/Nick Jr.
An imprint of Simon & Schuster Children's Publishing Divisic
New York   London   Toronto   Sydney   Singapc
1230 Avenue of the Americas, New York, New York 10020

Copyright © 2003 Viacom International Inc.
All rights reserved. NICKELODEON, NICK JR., and all related titles, logos, and
characters are trademarks of Viacom International Inc. Little Bill is a trademark of Smiley, Inc.
All rights reserved, including the right of reproduction in whole or in part in any form.
SIMON SPOTLIGHT and colophon are registered trademarks of Simon & Schuster.

Manufactured in China   First Edition   2 4 6 8 10 9 8 7 5 3 1   ISBN 0-689-85243-6

"What did one egg say to the other egg?" Little Bill asked his brother, Bobby.

"You crack me up," Bobby answered. "Little Bill, you told that joke last year."

"Last year *I* found the most eggs in the big Easter egg hunt," their sister, April, said. "And I'll do it again this year!"

"This year *I'm* going to find the *special* egg!" Little Bill exclaimed.

Dingdong! Little Bill and Alice the Great answered the door. It was Little Bill's cousin, Fuchsia, uncle Al, and aunt Vanessa.

"Well hello, Miss Lady. What a lovely hat," Alice the Great said to Fuchsia. "Thank you, Alice the Great. It's my special Easter bonnet—I only wear it once a year," replied Fuchsia.

It was time for the Easter egg hunt! "Who's ready to get down to business and find some eggs?" Big Bill called out.

"I'm going to find the special egg," Little Bill told Fuchsia. "It's wrapped in shiny paper and it's *all* chocolate! Every year the Easter Bunny hides it in a secret place, and this year I'm going to be the one to find it."

"*All* chocolate?" Fuchsia repeated. "I want to find the special egg too."

Little Bill and Fuchsia began hunting for the special egg.
First Fuchsia checked the mailbox. Maybe the Easter Bunny sent the special egg by special delivery, she thought.

"If I were the special egg," Little Bill said to himself, "I'd hide in the shade." He looked behind the tree, but only found a green egg hidden in the grass.

"Look how many eggs I found!" called Bobby, showing Fuchsia and
Little Bill his basket full of eggs. "How many do you have?"

"I'm only looking for the special egg," Little Bill told his brother.

"Me too!" Fuchsia exclaimed.

"But I'm going to find it first!" said Little Bill.

Then Alice the Great called them over to her.

"What's all this noise about being first? Maybe you two should try hunting for eggs together," said Alice the Great.

"I guess we could look together," replied Fuchsia.

"Yeah, together!" agreed Little Bill.

"Fuchsia, what happened to your Easter bonnet?" asked Alice the Great.

Fuchsia scratched her head and looked around the yard. "Oh, there it is, Alice the Great," she replied, pointing to her hat lying in the grass.

"Would you two please bring me that flowerpot right there next to it?" asked Alice the Great.

"Sure!" they exclaimed.

Together, Little Bill and Fuchsia lifted the flowerpot.
"It's the *special* egg! We found it! We found it together!" they cheered.

"Time for a picture!" Brenda called.

Everyone gathered around Fuchsia and Little Bill.

"Say, 'Happy Easter,' everyone!" Brenda told them.

"Happy Easter, everyone!" they shouted. And Little Bill and Fuchsia shouted loudest of all.